MANGLER
THE DARK MENACE

With special thanks to Michael Ford

For James McLaughlin

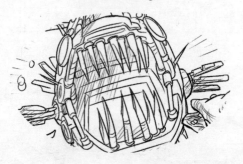

www.seaquestbooks.co.uk

ORCHARD BOOKS

First published in Great Britain in 2013 by Orchard Books
This edition published in 2016 by The Watts Publishing Group

5 7 9 10 8 6 4

Text © 2013 Beast Quest Limited.
Cover and inside illustrations by Artful Doodlers with special thanks to Bob and Justin
© Orchard Books 2013

Series created by Beast Quest Limited, London

The moral rights of the author and illustrator have been asserted.

A CIP catalogue record for this book is available from the British Library.

ISBN 978 1 40832 414 1

Printed in Great Britain by Clays Ltd, Elcograf S.p.A.

The paper and board used in this book are made from wood from responsible sources

Orchard Books
An imprint of Hachette Children's Group
Part of The Watts Publishing Group Limited
Carmelite House, 50 Victoria Embankment, London EC4Y 0DZ

An Hachette UK Company
www.hachette.co.uk
www.hachettechildrens.co.uk

MANGLER
THE DARK MENACE

BY ADAM BLADE

ORCHARD

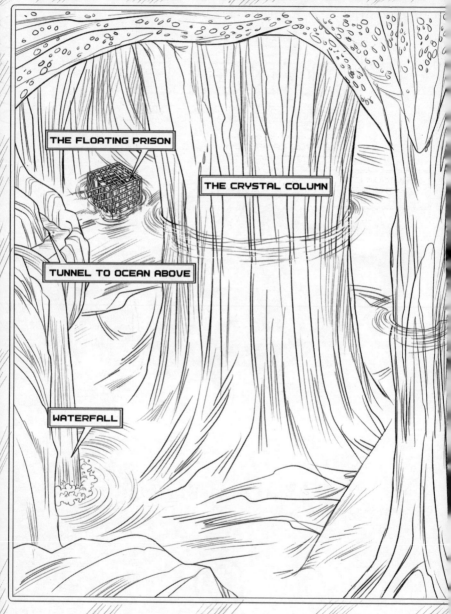

SPECTRON, 3,548 FATHOMS DEEP,
THE CAVERN OF GHOSTS

I've done it! At last I perfected my new invention. When the Professor strikes, I believe it could foil his evil plan…

Now I must find him. Someone has to stop him, and nobody knows him as well as I do. It will be hard to leave the Sea Ghosts unprotected. They are so kind and innocent, and have shared everything with me, all of their carefully collected treasures of the sea. I fear that they have even come to think of me as their guardian.

But I must leave if their world is to be saved. I can only hope that my new device will be enough to stop the Professor.

If it isn't, the Cavern of Ghosts — and everything that lies above — is doomed…

>LOG ENTRY ENDS

CHAPTER ONE

FISH FOOD

Sharp white peaks rose through the gloomy water as far as Max could see. They weren't mountains – they were enormous teeth. Max was staring into the mouth of the most gigantic sea creature he'd ever seen. Bigger than any ship built in his home city of Aquora, maybe even bigger than the city itself. A pink tongue thrust towards them, then slipped back into the black hole of the monster's throat.

"We're going to be swallowed!" Lia cried.

A rush of water gripped Max like a powerful undertow, sucking him through the water. He lost his grip on the aquabuggy and it spun away until it looked smaller than a child's toy.

"Swim for your lives!" said Roger. "Every sailor for himself!" He turned and swam against the current, boot-thrusters churning bubbles as he shot away.

Typical! thought Max.

"After him!" Lia shouted.

She clung close to Spike's back as the swordfish strained to fight the powerful surge of water. Rivet's leg propellers roared. Max kicked as hard as he could, but already he could feel that the current was too strong. Roger was a speck in the distance, but he seemed to be getting bigger again. *Even his thrusters aren't strong enough.*

"Hold, Max!" barked Rivet, as the current

dragged him down beside Max.

Max gripped his dogbot's collar, but he could feel the rush of water growing in strength like a gale. They were being sucked further into the creature's mouth, faster and faster.

It can't end like this! thought Max. *Not after*

everything we've done...

They'd just defeated Crusher, a giant robotic centipede built by Max's uncle, the evil Professor, but still the Sea Ghost city of Spectron wasn't safe. And neither was Sumara, the home of Lia's people, the Merryn. Their city was built right on top of this underwater cave world. If Max and Lia couldn't stop him, the Professor would destroy the crystal columns that supported the cavern roof. Then both cities would come toppling down.

Max's knuckles turned white on Rivet's collar, but they were losing ground. It was like being tugged backwards by an invisible hand.

"Swim harder, Riv!" he shouted.

Rivet's eyes flashed as he set his legs to maximum paddle. For a few moments, he managed to thrust his snout into the onrush of water, but then he fell back.

"It's no use," Lia called.

Max felt his hopes drain away. *We're all going to die.* He'd failed. The Professor was at large, and Max still didn't even know what had happened to his missing mother. Was she alive, somewhere in the oceans of Nemos? Could she really have been a pirate, like Roger had hinted?

They drifted past the first of the huge teeth. *Still time to fight our way out of this...*

"Latch on, boy!" Max shouted to Rivet.

His dogbot jerked sideways, and clamped his metal jaws onto one of the teeth. A horrible grating sound filled Max's ears as Riv's metal teeth slid across the surface. *It's not going to work!* But somehow, Rivet managed to cling on. Max looked back and saw that Spike had rammed his sword into the creature's gums. A beast this size probably wouldn't even feel it. Lia clung desperately to his back, her pale hair streaming out behind her.

Roger was heading towards them, feet first, as he lost his battle with the current.

"Help me!" he shouted through his mask's communication device.

"What happened to every sailor for himself?" called Max, as the water ripped through his hair and rushed past his eyes.

"Please!" yelled Roger.

"Grab onto me!" called Max, fighting to hold onto Rivet as he angled his body into Roger's path.

Roger tumbled over. Max reached out and grabbed his leg. The pirate managed to turn himself in the water and wrapped his arms around Max's waist. "Thanks, matey!" he called.

Max's shoulders burned from holding onto the collar and his fingers started to slip free.

I can't hold on any longer, he thought.

Then the water began to darken. Looking up, Max saw another set of colossal teeth descending. The great mouth was closing over them like sudden nightfall.

Everything went black, and the current slackened.

"Riv, switch on your snout lamp," said Max.

A red beam of light flashed up in the darkness. It cut through the gloom, picking out the terrified faces of the others.

Perhaps we'll be all right, after all, Max thought.

Then, with a sound like a waterfall, seawater began to gush into the creature's throat.

Roger's hands scrabbled and clawed at Max's clothes, but he was torn free. Max lost his grip on Rivet's collar and spun off into the dark. He saw Lia and Spike tumbling past as well. With a terrified whine, Rivet let go of

the tooth and plunged after his master. The
light from his snout lamp spun in dizzying
arcs.

I've got to do something! thought Max, as
huge teeth rushed past.

Rivet's whine rose in pitch, a panicked

sound just like the time he tried to eat a sea urchin, back home in the old days on the island city of Aquora. He'd coughed it up, eventually, when the spines tickled his throat.

Wait a minute...

Perhaps Max could do the same thing here, to make this creature cough them up!

He didn't have a sea urchin, but he had something better. As he rolled over and over in the current, Max reached to his belt and drew out his hyperblade. This huge monster would hardly feel it, but he only needed a tickle.

The great pink tongue passed beneath them, coated in strands of white slime. He saw Lia and Spike slip over the edge and disappear. Roger wailed as he fell after them. Max tried to grab the tongue to slow himself, but it was impossible. He trailed the hyperblade gently over the sickly-coloured flesh as he sped past.

It's got to work...

Suddenly, the whole creature shook, and Max was thrown forwards.

"He's gagging," Max muttered. He grabbed hold of the tongue and tickled it again with the hyperblade. Once more the creature coughed and he was hurled further from the throat's depths. Max ran the hyperblade across the tongue again, swishing it from side to side.

A roar began to build all around him. First Rivet, then Roger, and finally Lia and Spike shot from the darkness, their bodies flung towards him at incredible speed.

The current snatched Max and tossed him back the way they'd come. The water surged around Max's ears, louder than a jet engine. He felt his body buffeted against the side of a tooth. There was no fighting it.

Light returned, as the creature's huge mouth gaped open.

There was a choking roar, and Max and his friends were flung out into the open sea.

CHAPTER TWO

WAKING
THE GIANT

Max floated gently down to rest on the seabed. He checked over his body, but he couldn't find anything broken – just long strings of the sticky white goo that had coated the creature's tongue.

"Urgh!" He pulled a strand away from his gills, and tried to wipe it off his hands. It stank like rotten vegetables, and made him gag.

Lia was untangling herself from a clump of seaweed, and Spike was nosing beneath a boulder. He dragged Rivet by his tail from underneath the rock.

"Hey! Don't leave me!" called Roger.

Max looked back and saw the pirate snagged on the point of one of the teeth by his deepsuit. He was writhing to free himself.

"We could just forget about him," muttered Lia wearily.

Max grinned. He knew she wasn't completely serious. "Go get him, Riv," he said.

The dogbot cut through the water towards the tooth, and seized Roger's boot in his jaws. With a yank, he tore the adventurer free, leaving a shred of his deepsuit behind.

Roger swam over, scowling as he wiped the creature's dribble from his mask. Through the rip in his suit, Max made out a pair of underpants carrying a strange design. He bit his lip to hide a smile.

"Is that a skull and crossbones?" he said.

Roger squirmed to look over his shoulder, then covered the underwear with his hand. His cheeks flushed. "What if it is?"

"Very un-pirate-like," said Lia. Roger had always claimed that he wasn't a pirate, even though he looked – and behaved – just like one.

Lia's glance travelled upwards and beyond. "What is that thing?" she asked.

Max turned to face the creature and gasped. As the mouth slowly closed over the scarlet gums and mountain-range teeth, he could see it more clearly. It must have been as tall as the skyscraper he'd grown up in. Surely even the Professor couldn't build something so vast? This didn't look like a robot, anyway. Its skin was mottled and grey, like ancient, weather-beaten stone. It might have looked like a giant slug, or a whale, but no whale ever grew this size. *Can it even swim?* Max wondered. *Or does it just lie here like a wrecked sub?* Max couldn't make out

any eyes, but they might be somewhere on the creature's upper reaches, way out of sight.

With a groaning sound that shook Max's bones, the creature shuddered. Its skin shifted just a fraction, but the shockwave was enough to send Max and the others tumbling. Rivet barked: "Big fish wake up!"

As Roger clambered to his feet beside Max,

he frowned. "Dorminus is no fish," he said.

"Dorminus?" said Max.

"And it never wakes," said Roger, but he looked uncertain.

The water shook again as the creature twitched, but this time Max managed to keep his footing.

"It looks like he's waking now," said Max, "so

how about you tell us what he is?"

"It's not a he," said Roger, "or a she. It's an it, and I can't believe you've never heard of the One Who Sleeps."

"I have," said Lia quietly, "but I thought it was a myth. Dorminus, the One Who Sleeps – the foundation of the sea."

"Okay," said Max. "So everyone else knows about this Dorminus, which isn't a fish, and never wakes. But what is he? I mean, 'it'?"

"No one knows," said Roger. "It's been here for thousands of years, since before the Sea Ghosts even reached this part of the ocean."

Another tremor shook the sea as the beast shifted. Clouds of sand rose from the seabed, swirling around them. Max covered his eyes until it settled. Rivet shook sand off his back.

"So maybe it is waking up," said Roger.

"It must be the Professor's doing," said Max. He thought of the strange skin they'd found beneath the Sea Ghost city, and the heartbeat that echoed within. It had to be part of this creature. Suddenly he realised. "If Dorminus stirs, Spectron will be destroyed," he said.

Roger took a deep breath. "Not just Spectron," he said. "Sumara too. The crystal columns won't hold if Dorminus hits them."

Lia's face was pale. "Then we have to stop him waking. But how?"

"We find the Professor," said Max grimly. "Why else would Dorminus be waking now? My uncle must be behind it – we know he means to take control of the whole ocean, and only he would try something like this."

He swam quickly to Rivet and opened the dogbot's back compartment. Inside was the black box they'd taken from Stinger the Sea Phantom. Max switched it on, with Lia peering over his shoulder. A three-dimensional map was projected in the water, glowing green.

At first, Max couldn't even tell what he was looking at. He twisted the rangefinder. The map zoomed out, and gradually the outline of the enormous beast could be seen. Max gasped at the sheer size of the creature. It looked a bit like a giant sea slug, with a snub nose, a forked tail and a number of great fins. Near the first of the fins, on top of the Beast, was a green

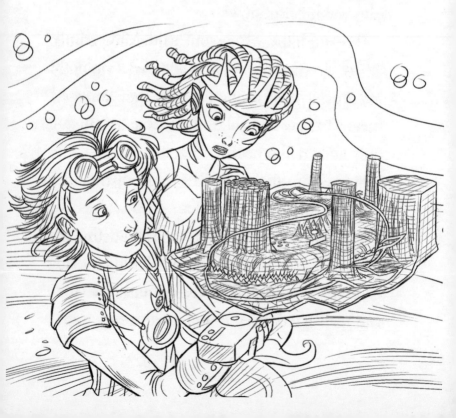

flashing dot. *The Professor!*

"There he is," said Max, his suspicions confirmed. "It's time we faced him again."

"What are those?" asked Lia, pointing to a series of rectangles positioned along Dorminus's flanks.

Max peered closer, but couldn't make out any detail. One thing was for sure. "They look man-made," he said.

The map flickered as Dorminus's huge bulk shifted a fraction. The sea shook violently and tossed them sideways as if they weighed nothing. Max fetched up against a boulder and rubbed his head dizzily. He spotted his aquabuggy a short distance away, nestled in a patch of seaweed.

"We can't stay here," said Roger, adjusting his face mask. "One of these tremors could kill us."

"And we can't cross Dorminus's surface," said Lia. "It'll be like trying to run a race in the middle of an earthquake."

Max swam towards the aquabuggy. "Help me with this," he called to the others.

With Lia and Rivet pushing from below and Roger helping to tug from above, they managed to flip the buggy over in the water. Max thumped the ignition and the control panel lit up. *At least it's still working.* "Maybe we should stick close to the sea floor," said Max, "by Dorminus's side. The disturbances shouldn't be as bad there."

Roger gulped. "What if he rolls over? We'll be flatter than ship's biscuits."

"You don't have to come," said Lia.

"I didn't say I wouldn't," said Roger. "I just want to know the risks, that's all."

As Lia and Roger traded insults, Max found the piece of shell they'd retrieved from Crusher the Creeping Terror – a metal segment with a sword-like leg. He got out a thermal welder, and fastened the shell to the rear thruster of the buggy with the spike protruding.

"What are you doing?" asked Lia.

"It should help keep us stable in the currents," said Max, hopping into the driver's seat.

Lia clicked her tongue, and Spike swam over and underneath her legs so she could climb onto his back. Roger was stabbing at the thruster controls on his wrist. "Some sort of malfunction," he said.

Max rolled his eyes. Roger would do anything to avoid danger. "Well, jump on board," he said.

The pirate gave a weak smile as he shifted into the seat beside Max. "What are we waiting for?" he said. "Raise the anchor!"

Max took the handlebars, and pressed the accelerator. The buggy scooted across the seabed, towards Dorminus's colossal form.

"We're coming to get you, Uncle," Max muttered under his breath.

CHAPTER THREE

A SHOCKING DISCOVERY

Max had never felt so small. Dorminus seemed to go on forever. *We're like plankton crawling along the side of a whale,* thought Max. The beast's grey, scarred skin was covered in patches of sea moss and barnacles. Shoals of fish nibbled at its hide. Max kept his eyes peeled for any sign of movement. If the huge looming mass even shifted, he was ready to streak away. Lia glided at one side on Spike, with Rivet paddling on the other.

Max checked the black box every so often, and saw they were approaching the first of the mysterious rectangles. Suddenly, through the shadows ahead, he saw one and slowed. It was about the size of his aquabuggy, a mass of cabling housed in a steel shell and stuck into Dorminus's side. From the broken flesh, Max guessed the objects had been added recently. *By the Professor, no doubt.*

"How cruel!" said Lia. "No wonder Dorminus is waking up – he must be in so much pain."

"That uncle of yours is crazy," said Roger, "messing with something this size."

"We should try and detach it," said Max. "Then hopefully Dorminus will sleep again."

Lia left Spike and swam closer. Max followed. He saw that there were several clasps fastening the housing in place. Lia

reached for the first with her webbed fingers.
"This shouldn't be too—"

"Don't touch it!" yelled Max.

But it was too late. A spark flashed to her
hand and she jolted backwards with a cry.

"Lia!" Max shouted.

His Merryn friend hung limply in the water, her hair trailing over her face. Max swam over to her as fast as he could, supported her slumped body and gently turned her over.

"Is she dead?" whispered Roger.

Max didn't dare answer. He stroked the hair from her face. Lia's eyes were closed, and there was a nasty burn on her hand. "I can't lose you too," Max whispered. "Not after everything we've been through."

"Scared, Max!" barked Rivet.

Spike swam closer and gave Lia's ribs a gentle nudge with the side of his bill. She didn't flinch. The swordfish backed away, letting out a series of high-pitched squeaks.

"Move aside," said Roger. He was opening a pouch at his belt, and took out what looked like a pink snail shell. At once, Max's nostrils picked up an awful smell, like fish left in the sun too long, but a hundred times worse.

"Trust me," said Roger, and he held the shell beneath Lia's nose. After a second or two, her eyelids fluttered and then opened.

Roger grinned. "Stinksnail," he said. "The Grundle swear by it."

Relief flooded through Max. He held his nose. "Just put it away!" he said.

The pirate did as he was asked, and Lia shook her head weakly from side to side. She tucked her injured hand into her armpit. Spike did a vertical spin in the water, waving his sword with pleasure.

"Are you okay, Lia?" asked Max.

"I think so," she said, her voice slightly slurred. "It was horrible..."

Max looked back at the metal clasps. And suddenly he understood his uncle's plan. "Electric shocks – the Professor must be using them to wake up Dorminus! Huge shocks – much bigger than the one you just got."

Lia's eyes widened, and she clambered back onto Spike. "Then we have to stop him," she said. "Come on!"

Max admired her courage. She seemed to have forgotten about her injured hand as they set out, and raced alongside Dorminus. The water grew darker, and soon Max had to switch on the aquabuggy's headlights. Rivet nosed ahead of them, his own snout lamp throwing out a cone of light into the dim ocean. Max dreaded to think what surprises the Professor might have in store, lurking in the darkness.

They reached the first side fin before long. It hung in the water like a giant grey sail, its edges fading into the distance. Max checked the black box map.

"The Professor's still up there," he said, pointing towards the creature's back. "We've got him!" *Unless he knows we're coming...*

"Good luck, everyone," said Roger. For once he looked deadly serious.

Max nodded and angled the buggy upwards. They began to scale the massive flank of the beast. No one spoke for a long time, and the only sound was the soft hum of the buggy's thrusters.

"Are you sure this is right?" said Lia after a few moments.

Max checked the depth gauge. They were climbing fast, but it was still dark, and the top of the creature seemed no nearer. Then at last the grey hulk of its body started to curve away. As they glided over the top they saw dotted blue lights shining below, covering Dorminus's skin like stars, connected with a fine mesh of wires.

"I wonder what they're for," said Lia.

For a split second, the blue lights flared brighter. Then the buggy's lights died, along with Rivet's snout lamp, throwing them into darkness. Max pressed the headlight switch several times, but nothing happened.

"They must have sent out some sort of electronic pulse," he said. "It's killed our lights."

"So much for sneaking up," said Roger.

They drifted in the dark sea, lit only by the blue lights below, until Rivet let out a low growl. His eyes glowed a dull red as he pointed his nose along Dorminus's back. There, like a distant comet, was a single white light. It grew larger and brighter as it moved towards them.

"Looks like we've been spotted," said Max. "Something's coming for us."

CHAPTER FOUR

THE DARK MENACE

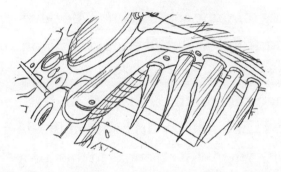

"Is it the Professor?" asked Lia.

Max tried to activate the black box to find out, but it didn't work. It must have been wiped out by the strange electronic pulse.

Suddenly the light blinked off. When it reappeared again, a moment later, it had moved sideways by fifty paces. *Whatever it is, it's fast...* thought Max.

The light flashed on and off several times. Rivet began to bark.

"Calm down, boy," said Max, swimming off his seat towards his dogbot. "What's wrong?"

The glowing light stuttered again, in long and short bursts, and Max realised it was giving off some sort of signal. *Morse code?* He couldn't follow it well enough – no one used Morse any more – but then he remembered he had programmed Rivet to understand it. He was about to lay his hand on the dogbot's collar, when Rivet engaged his propellers and zoomed away. Right towards the light!

"Rivet coming!"

"Riv, wait!" shouted Max.

The flashing light continued to throw out its signal. *The Morse code must be messing with his command circuits.*

Max leaped back into the aquabuggy's seat and gunned the engine. Roger lurched backwards as they sped through the water.

"Steady on, matey!" he said. Without

headlamps, Max was just following the flashing light ahead. He found the trailing bubbles of Rivet's wake and pressed the pedal to the floor. But Rivet was fast too.

"Careful, Max!" called Lia. "It might be a trap."

That's why I have to rescue Riv, he thought. *The Professor can wait.* As the pulsing light grew closer, Max's heart began to thump harder in his chest. He could see now that it was an eye, attached to a flexible metal stalk. And the stalk was connected to the forehead of a huge robotic creature. It looked like an angler fish, its body narrow but almost perfectly circular from the side, like a coin. But a coin fifty times the size of Rivet, and glinting with cold steel. A nameplate had been bolted to the creature's side. It read 'MANGLER'. The Robobeast's jaws gaped, revealing metal spikes instead of teeth. It

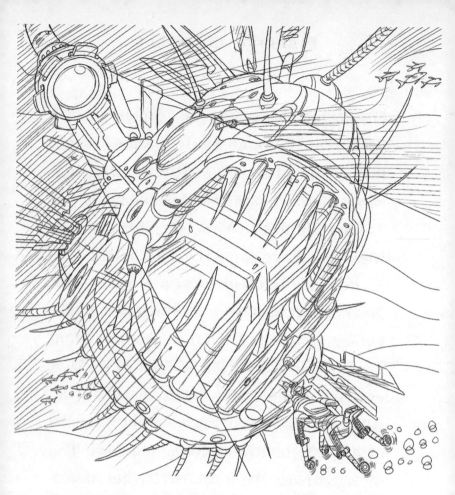

could have swallowed the aquabuggy in a
single mouthful.

It had to be the work of the Professor. And
Rivet was heading straight for it, tail wagging
in excitement, mesmerised by the light.

Max felt like he was seeing it in slow motion.

His dogbot swam between Mangler's teeth. With a horrible sound of screeching metal, they slammed shut. But Riv was titanium alloy, one of the toughest metals known in Aquora. The teeth had met their match. Rivet whined as they clamped over his middle. The jaws opened and slammed down again. This time they didn't let go. Rivet's rear end was wriggling as he tried to free himself from the iron grip. Max saw the hinges of the jaws grinding up and down.

He won't last long!

Max snatched up the long hyperblade he'd salvaged from Shredder the Spider Droid. But before he could kick off, someone grabbed hold of the blade and yanked it out of his hands.

Max squirmed around and saw Roger, brandishing the hyperblade and grinning.

"Allow me to lead the way," he said. "I owe

that mutt of yours a favour."

Roger engaged his boot-thrusters and flashed ahead.

Max swam after him. *I can't let him tackle this alone.*

Roger reached the Robobeast first, and raised the hyperblade. The eye-stalk swivelled towards him and a blaster beam hissed through the water, lighting up the scene for an instant. It zapped the hyperblade and sent it spinning out of Roger's hand. Max hurled himself at Roger, pushing him out of the way as another beam shot towards him. It missed by a fraction and struck Dorminus's thick hide.

A tremor rumbled around them, picking Max and Roger up and spinning them over in cartwheels. Max found himself alone, behind their new attacker, but with a flash Mangler turned to face him. Max cast around and saw the hyperblade drifting nearby. He grabbed hold of it and raised it just as another blaster beam scorched towards him from the robot's eye. His arms shook as the hyperblade absorbed the blow.

Sheltering behind his weapon, he approached the Robobeast, which was thrashing its head from side to side as it tried to chew down on Rivet. The dogbot howled, and already one of his back legs was dangling. *He must have severed a circuit*, thought Max. Desperation gnawed at his stomach. Rivet had been his loyal companion for so long. *If we don't rescue him soon, he'll just be nuts and bolts.*

Another blaster beam shot towards Max, and he ducked and felt the water sizzle over his head. Roger had vanished, but Max couldn't blame him this time. He was fifty paces from the Robobeast, and it was hard to see how he could get any closer. Max swam back and forth as he approached, and the eye tracked him. Was the Professor watching somewhere, through a monitor? *He's waiting for the perfect shot*, thought Max. *And I can't let him get it.*

Max threw himself at the head-sized eye. A blaster shot flashed past, missing him by a hair's breadth. He raised the hyperblade and swung it at the orb. The blow was only a glancing one, but Mangler shuddered, twitched and withdrew a little way.

I hurt it...

Max went after the Robobeast, raising his weapon for another strike. But Mangler twisted in the water. Too late, Max saw the tail. It slammed into him like a wet metal wall, knocking the wind from his lungs and sending him sprawling into Dorminus's rough flank. He let go of the hyperblade.

His head was spinning as he fought to draw water through his gills.

Through his blurred vision he saw Lia had joined the attack, on Spike. She jerked this way and that, dodging the blaster beams. Lia was too quick for Mangler, but Max knew she would tire soon. Rivet had stopped struggling and hung from the pincer grip of the beast's teeth.

Is it too late?

While Lia and her swordfish were keeping Mangler busy, a shape appeared above the beast.

Roger!

The pirate was stalking slowly through the water, and he was clutching the hyperblade Max had dropped. He hovered for a moment, right above the deadly creature's eye, and gave Max a wink with his one good eye. Then he tipped forward headfirst.

"He's mad..." muttered Max.

"Ahoy there, rusty chops!" Roger bellowed.

Mangler stopped attacking Lia and his eye swivelled upwards. At the same time, Roger's boot-thrusters sped him towards Mangler's jaws. He rammed the hyperblade between them. The eye rotated, trying to fix a shot,

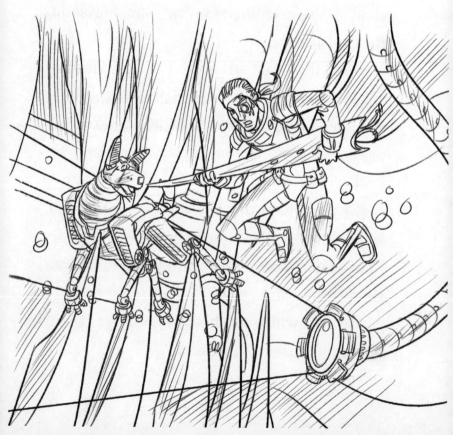

but Roger was too close. With a heave, he levered the hyperblade and the jaws creaked open. Rivet floated free, and his leg propellers carried him slowly out of harm's way.

"Sorry, Max!" he barked weakly. Now the beast was no longer flashing his code, Rivet seemed back to his normal self.

Mangler clamped down on the hyperblade, and thrashed it from Roger's grip. With a crunch, the beast snapped it in half, leaving the pieces drifting down towards Dorminus. *No! Roger's defenceless now!* Max kicked off towards the pirate, but there was no way he could reach him in time. Roger threw up a hand, as if to protect himself, but Mangler lunged forward.

Its jaws came slicing down over Roger's forearm.

The pirate howled in pain.

CHAPTER FIVE

A PIRATE'S DESTINY

"Help him, Spike!" Lia shouted.

"Aim for the eye!" cried Max. It had to be the Robobeast's weak spot.

The swordfish skimmed away from beneath his Merryn rider and dived towards the beast. Mangler was too focused on Roger to notice, and Spike drove his sword into the spot where the eye-stalk met the metal body. The swordfish thrashed and stabbed deeper, tail thumping against the beast's face.

Several blaster bolts shot aimlessly through the water, and smoke bubbles burst from the wound. Mangler gave an electronic squeal.

The beast's metal jaws sprang open and Roger kicked away, clutching his wrist. Blood swirled around him in the water. Max couldn't see how bad the injury was, but he feared the worst. No flesh and bone could stand up to those teeth.

Mangler twitched, its tail flapping and its body jerking wildly. There was a flash as the eye-blaster exploded, showering debris through the water. Spike was thrown clear, his sword still tangled in wires. With an ear-splitting screech, the Robobeast flipped around and swam away at speed. In a moment, they were alone.

Max felt no sense of triumph, only relief that the threat was gone.

Roger drifted beside the aquabuggy,

groaning and clutching his wrist. Max swam over, but Lia got there first. "Here, let me," she said gently.

She took some of the wiring from Spike's sword, and quickly tied it tightly above the wound, just beneath Roger's elbow. "That should stop the bleeding."

"My hand! My hand!" Roger was saying. His face was white as coral. With a gasp, Max saw that the pirate's hand was completely gone, leaving nothing beyond his torn deepsuit sleeve.

With the loop of wire in place, the bleeding slowed to a trickle. At least the salt in the seawater would stop any infection.

"It hurts!" said Roger.

"Here, take this," Lia replied. She fished in her knapsack and drew out what looked like a speckled pebble. "It's cloudstone. You suck it. It will dull the pain."

Roger sucked furiously on the pebble, and even managed a thin smile.

"New hand!" barked Rivet, from somewhere nearby.

"Not now," said Max. "Roger's badly injured."

"New hand!" Rivet said again. His propellers carried him closer, and Max saw that one leg still dangled uselessly from a torn joint. Rivet was clutching something in his jaw. It was the pointed end of the hyperblade from Shredder the Spider Droid, its edges curled where Mangler had bitten it in two.

"What does he mean, 'new hand?'" said Roger.

Max understood at once. "Good thinking, Riv," he said.

He took out Rivet's toolkit and went to work with his thermo welder, sitting on the side of the aquabuggy out of sight of the

others. Luckily, the metal of the hyperblade was easy to work.

"It's going to be fine," Lia told Roger.

Max attached an arm clasp to his creation, so that the new hand would sit properly in place of the old one.

"Pirate save Rivet," barked the dogbot. "Thank you, pirate!"

"Yes, I suppose I did," said Roger proudly. "But I'm not a... Oh, never mind."

Max stowed away the tools and approached the others. He held out the twist of metal, shaped into a perfect hook.

"You cannot be serious," said Roger. "You expect me to wear that?"

Max smiled. "Sorry. It's the best I can do."

Roger narrowed his eyes. "Very well," he said. He held out his stump and turned his face away, his eyes screwed shut. "Do your worst."

Max felt a little sick as he carefully positioned the hooked hand over the wrist, but he was pleased with the fit. Roger was silent throughout the delicate operation, though Max could feel his arm trembling. He felt awful – every movement must have been causing Roger terrible pain. *But this is the best thing we can do for him right now.* As he closed the fastenings, Max muttered: "There, done. You might have a little more trouble convincing people you're not a pirate now. But at least you've got a hand."

Roger lifted his hook in front of his face and stared at Max's handiwork. Max couldn't tell if he was going to cry or laugh. *It does look a bit makeshift.* At last, a slow smile crept across Roger's lips. "Arrr," he whispered. Then, louder: "Arrrr!"

Lia was smiling too. "It's time to stop pretending, Roger."

Roger stood up, and kicked off the aquabuggy's seat into open water. He swished the hook back and forth. "ARRR!"

"Are you all right, Roger?" asked Max. "Maybe it's time to spit out that cloudstone."

But Roger only grinned wider. "That's

Captain Roger to you, me hearty! Cap'n Jolly Roger, scourge of the Seven Seas!"

"Well, Captain," said Lia, laughing. "Are you ready to set sail?"

"Aye, me lassie. I'm all shipshape now. Let's weigh anchor and..."

Another tremor swallowed his words. The ocean shook fiercely, and a deep groan rose from the sea floor. Max grabbed the aquabuggy's controls, and Rivet trembled.

"Dorminus," said Lia. "We haven't got long!"

"Leave this pillaging Professor to me," said Roger, with another swat of his hook. "I'll have him keel-hauled. I'll make him walk the plank. I'll give him a taste of the cat-o'—"

"Yes, that's great," said Lia, "but first we need to deal with *that*!"

She pointed behind Roger, and Max saw the dark shape of Mangler cruising through the water towards them. It no longer had its blaster eye, but its gnashing teeth looked as sharp as ever. And it was back for more.

CHAPTER SIX

MANGLER'S REVENGE

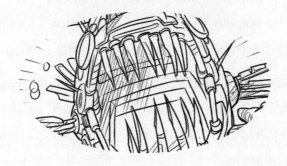

M ax looked at each of his companions in turn. With Shredder's blade gone, they only had one weapon left – Max's own, handheld hyperblade. He drew it and brandished it in front of him.

I might as well have a toothpick, he thought.

This was a fight they couldn't win.

"Should we run?" asked Lia.

Roger swiped his hook at the approaching creature. "Turn tail? Not this pirate. That beastie took my hand. I'll have revenge!"

"Anyway, Mangler's too quick for us," Max added. "It'd chase us down."

Rivet whined.

The robotic monster was stalking closer, its body flashing from side to side. The remains of its smashed blaster-eye hung from its socket. *At least it's only the teeth we have to deal with now*, Max thought. But that wasn't much consolation.

"Wait, Max," said Lia. "We do have a weapon we could use."

Max tore his eyes from Mangler and flashed a look at his Merryn friend. "I'm not sure Roger's hook or my hyperblade are going to be enough."

"No," said Lia. "That conch shell the Sea Ghost gave you. The one that was your mother's."

Max reached under his tunic and drew out the strange shell. His dad had had one just like it decorating his desk in Aquora. But this shell was different – it had wiring and circuitry embedded deep in its swirls.

"But we have no idea what it does," he said. "It doesn't look like a weapon."

Mangler was pressing closer. With its jaws parted, it seemed to be grinning. Hungrily.

"Well, there's only one way to find out,

laddie," said Roger. "Blow it!"

Max lifted the shell to his lips, then paused. "What if does something awful? What if it scrambles our brains, or even wakes Dorminus? Then we're in trouble."

Mangler snapped his teeth.

"And what are we in now?" asked Lia.

She's right, thought Max. *It's our only hope.*

Roger had told Max that his mother wasn't just a simple explorer – he'd hinted that she was a pirate too. But Max knew he had to trust her. She wouldn't have built anything that would destroy a whole world.

Would she?

"Quick, Max!" said Lia. Mangler was going to reach them within seconds.

Max lifted the conch shell in a trembling hand. He took a deep breath and put the shell to his lips. *Here goes nothing...*

"Fish!" barked Rivet suddenly. "Fish! Fish!"

Max lowered the shell. "What is it, Riv?"

His dogbot was pointing his nose into the distance. There, beyond Mangler, Max spotted a line of glowing lights dancing eerily in the water. But what sort of fish were they?

"There are more," said Lia. "Look!"

She pointed with her webbed hand to their right, where another shoal of glowing creatures was drifting through the water towards them.

"We're surrounded," said Roger, jerking his hook to the left.

Sure enough, more creatures were closing in. Mangler had paused in the water, flashing its head back and forth to take in the new arrivals.

As the shapes moved closer, Max began to recognise the outlines – heads, legs and arms – and dim, almost transparent features.

"They're not fish," he said. Hope surged up in his heart. "It's the Sea Ghosts of Spectron!"

CHAPTER SEVEN
A FIGHT TO THE DEATH

Max slipped the conch shell back under his tunic as he spotted Ko swimming towards him. The Sea Ghost had his mother Allis with him, now fully recovered from her fever. Before, her outline had been a dull jade, but now it glowed bright emerald green. "What are you doing here?" asked Max.

Ko waved a hand towards his people. "You help us defend our world, Max," he said. "Now we defend you."

Max was so grateful he thought he might burst. Ko had betrayed them once, when the Professor had his mother imprisoned. But he had a good heart.

"I can't let you do that," he said. "Your people will get hurt."

A wave of Sea Ghost thoughts washed over Max, as they communicated with their minds.

We're not scared any more...

Let us help...

This creature is no match for us...

Roger shook his hook. "Arrr!"

Ko looked slightly alarmed. "He all right?"

Lia shrugged. "He's just getting in touch with his inner pirate."

Mangler gnashed his teeth in a grinding metal snarl.

"Warriors of Spectron, attack!" shouted Ko.

Like a giant swarm of glowing green bees, the Sea Ghosts darted in at Mangler from three sides. The Robobeast snapped at one group, but they fluttered effortlessly aside. The metal teeth closed on nothing but water.

Another stream of Sea Ghosts, led by Ko, poured around its head, batting it with their fists. Mangler streaked after them, jaws gaping.

Ko broke away from the others, and Mangler trailed at his feet, snapping and snapping.

He's going to get eaten! thought Max.

Ko was almost inside Mangler's mouth when he jerked sideways with astonishing speed. The Robobeast twisted in the water, obviously confused about where its meal had gone.

A patch of glowing Sea Ghosts appeared just ahead of it. Mangler lunged towards them, only for the lights to go out at once.

"Where've they gone?" asked Lia.

A second later, the lights reappeared, a short distance from the robot predator. It launched forwards again, but once more, the Sea Ghost shoal did their disappearing act. Almost instantly, lights appeared all over Mangler's metal shell, hammering it with their fists and feet. It shook them off, writhing in the water.

"They're tiring it out," said Roger.

Sparks fizzed from the dangling wires on

Mangler's head, and its body jerked. "I don't think its circuits are quite right," said Max. *But the Sea Ghosts couldn't defeat it on their own. How can we finish it off?*

Mangler pursued a host of Sea Ghosts close to Dorminus. As they dodged one of the electrical hubs that had hurt Lia, Max had an idea.

"What if we used the Professor's tech against his own creation?" he said. "If we could throw Mangler onto one of those hubs and give it an electric shock..."

"Perfect!" said Lia. "But how can we catch it?"

"We need a harpoon," said Roger.

Max swam quickly to the aquabuggy, eyes on Crusher's shell with its spike. *It's not a harpoon, but it might work as a tow rope.* Above, he saw Ko and a bunch of Sea Ghosts streaming towards them. Mangler was hot on their heels.

Max leaped up to the aquabuggy's controls and brought up the computer display. Most buggies had some sort of magnetic grippers. Maybe he could reroute the circuitry to magnetise Crusher's body part... The Sea Ghosts parted suddenly and Mangler shot between them, snapping in frustration.

Max found what he was looking for. A few circuit tweaks, and Crusher's segment thrummed with power. Roger shot through the water, hook outstretched, and clamped onto the link. The magnet was just as strong as Max had hoped.

"Hey, what's going on?" asked Roger.

Max switched off the power, and Roger floated free. "You'd better stay clear," said Max.

"Hey!" Lia called.

Max glanced up to see Mangler, surrounded by darting Sea Ghosts. But the Robobeast didn't seem bothered by them any more. It was facing Lia, who hovered in the water. It began to move slowly, intently, towards her.

"I'm coming!" yelled Max.

He leaped into the buggy's seat, Rivet at his side, and gunned the engine towards his friends. Mangler put on a burst of speed too, jaws creaking open. Max floored the buggy's pedal and activated the magnets. Lia pushed Spike away from her. "Go!" she said. But the brave swordfish wouldn't leave her side.

Mangler closed in, fast. So did Max from underneath. But he could already see that the Robobeast would get to his friends first.

As he zoomed through the water, Max heaved the buggy to one side. At the same moment, Lia screamed. With a metallic clang, the magnetic link clamped onto Mangler's tail and stopped it dead in the water. Metal teeth snapped a hair's breadth from the Merryn girl.

"Gotcha!" yelled Max. He pushed the thrusters to full and heaved the beast away from his friend. The engines roared.

I hope Crusher's link holds...

The Sea Ghosts had all backed away, watching as Max towed Mangler through the water. The Professor's creature was thrashing madly, churning up bubbles as it tried to free itself from the magnetic grip.

"Go, Max!" yelled Lia.

"You've caught yourself a whopper there!" called Roger.

The buggy's panel flashed a warning – the engines were overheating. He didn't have much time. Max steered towards the nearest metal hub embedded in Dorminus's side, dragging his catch. It seemed like Mangler understood, because it began to struggle even more, shaking the buggy and making it hard to stay seated. Max gritted his teeth. *Oh no you don't...* he thought. *Time to fry this fish!*

He skirted the sleeping giant's flank and then rose away, switching off the magnets. Looking back, he saw Mangler tossed towards the studs. The beast's momentum carried it right into the patch of electrified cables.

BOOOOOOM!!!

A shockwave gripped Max and the buggy and threw him clear. As a flash of light burst through the water, he saw the Sea Ghosts,

tossed like leaves in the wind. He heard Rivet's high whine, and Spike's squeaks of fear.

When he righted himself, the buggy was drifting upside down a short distance away. Smoke trails and pieces of metal debris were hanging in the water. One part looked suspiciously like Mangler's tail.

Max struck out, looking for his friends. If

they hadn't made it, this would all have been for nothing... Then he saw them, drifting in the water and unharmed.

"You did it!" Lia cried. "Mangler's finished!"

"Arrr!" roared Roger.

Hurray! cried several of the Sea Ghosts.

But Max didn't have time to celebrate. A sudden mighty force seemed to suck at and push on his body at the same time. It was like the ocean was heaving in a giant breath. Another *BOOM* and he was hurled sideways. Then another, this time a series of rumbles that shook him in the water. The Sea Ghosts' flickering forms quivered as one.

More explosions?

Max looked down through a blur of bubbles that rose from the ocean floor. Then he understood and his blood ran cold.

"Oh no," he whispered. "We've woken it. Dorminus. The One Who Sleeps is awake!"

CHAPTER EIGHT

THE PROFESSOR

Max swam to the buggy, hopped on and scooted over to his friends. Currents smashed into the small craft, but he held his course.

There was no sending Dorminus back to sleep now.

A strong wave knocked him sideways as he got near to Roger, but the pirate managed to latch his hook over the seat and drag himself on board. Lia had mounted Spike and kept a firm grip over his neck. "Let's get out of here," she said.

"Agreed," said Max. "Ready, Riv?"

The dogbot barked in agreement.

With the Sea Ghosts trailing in their wake, Max climbed higher over Dorminus's shifting flank. It looked more like rock than skin, or the battle-scarred hull of an ancient steel ship, with pockmarks of sea-moss. He tried to keep a straight course through the buffeting water, and at last they reached the top of the giant creature. Here the mesh of blue lights glowed dimly again, but something had changed. About five hundred paces away, right in the centre of Dorminus's back, a red glare lit up the water. Some sort of pod. Max had no doubt who lurked inside, and his blood boiled.

The Professor.

He guided the buggy closer, and gradually

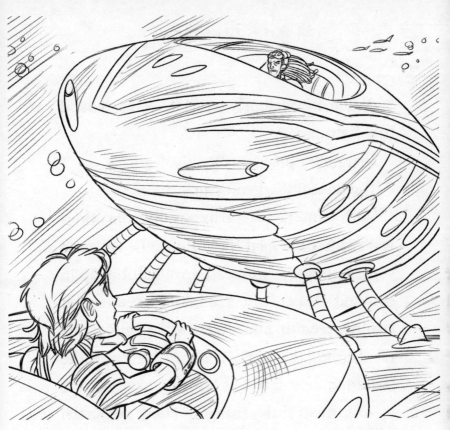

the pod's outline became clear. It was made of sleek titanium, slightly pointed towards the tip for smooth movement through the water. Strip lights blinked along its sides, and there were hatches below them. *Blaster cannons, probably*, thought Max. At the front, a viewing panel blinked into life, and a face glared through. A face with chill blue eyes staring viciously at Max. A hard face, full of cruelty.

His uncle's face.

The face of the Professor.

Max paused a few buggy-lengths away, where he could hear the soft purr of the pod's stabilisers. "We've defeated your Robobeast," shouted Max. The sea shuddered under another tremor, and his knuckles were white on the buggy's handlebars as he fought to steady it.

"Oh, that little thing," called back the Professor, his voice booming through the pod's speakers. "That was just an appetiser. Here comes the real show! You've kindly woken Dorminus for me. And when he smashes the crystal columns that hold up the Cavern of Ghosts, nothing can save this world or the one above. Spectron will be ruined, then Sumara! Then, who knows, I might take Dorminus to Aquora. He'll sink those skyscrapers beneath the waves with a flick of his tail!"

The Sea Ghosts gathered at Max's back. "We deal with him," Ko said. "Must stand up to bully."

Before Max could say anything, the Sea Ghosts surged towards the pod. But the Professor just smiled. Max saw his fingers flicking over the controls. The pod's rear end opened up and dozens of egg shapes shot into the open water. Each one trailed snaking arms ending in cruel grappling hooks.

Attack Bots...

The Sea Ghosts swarmed all over the deadly droids. The water swirled and bubbled as they darted and dodged. Max heard several cry out in pain, but others managed to grip the Attack Bots' tentacles and drag them down through the water.

Another tremor shook the sea as Dorminus shifted. This time his entire body seemed to lift a little in the water. It was a strange feeling, like the whole ground rippling beneath them. A grinding sound rattled Max's bones. He realised the giant was moving sideways over the ocean floor, dragging them along in its slipstream.

"Oh no!" said Lia.

By the eerie light of the swirling Sea Ghosts, Max saw what she was looking at. Crystal shards, like giant snowflakes, were drifting down through the water.

The crystal columns!

"One of the columns must already be crumbling," said Max.

"Some of the columns have grown on Dorminus itself," said Roger. "They won't hold for long."

That meant that the Cavern of Ghosts –

and Sumara above it – could be destroyed at any moment. *We're in big trouble now*, Max thought.

The Sea Ghosts were still furiously battling the Attack Bots. Max couldn't tell who was coming out on top, through the swirling currents. A few of the Ghosts were backing away, clutching injuries, but at least two of the Attack Bots had been ripped to pieces as well.

The Professor's cackles filled the water. "Not long now, my nephew! Soon the Cavern of Ghosts will crumble!"

Max remembered listening to Dorminus's heartbeat in Spectron. The Sea Ghost city had been built right on top of the huge creature. *If Dorminus is moving, what does that mean? Is it already too late to save the city?*

Through the water, an enormous shape loomed, glowing white. It stretched from the sea floor vertically into the water, disappearing in the ocean's upper reaches like an enormous tree trunk.

"It's the foundation column," said Lia. "The one that supports Sumara."

She ducked away as an Attack Bot flailed at her with a hook.

And Dorminus was shifting, slowly but surely, towards the column.

Max's heart sank. The Professor wasn't

just using the electric shock hubs to wake Dorminus – he was using them to drive him towards the column. *It's his biggest Robobeast yet!* Nothing could stop this moving mountain. No weapon was large enough to even make a scratch in its hide.

Unless...

Through the chaos of the battle between Sea Ghosts and Attack Bots, Max spied his uncle's pod. If he could get inside, perhaps he could switch off the electric shockers. It might not send Dorminus back to sleep straight away. But if it stopped him moving towards the column, that was a start.

Max snatched up his hyperblade, leaped off the buggy and swam towards his uncle.

"What are you doing?" yelled Lia. "Are you crazy?"

"If I fail, you've got to swim away fast," said Max. "Go to Sumara and warn them."

"Come back!" barked Rivet. "Danger!"

"Sorry, boy," said Max.

More Attack Bots swept in. Roger slashed at one with his hook. "Take that, scallywag!"

Another, already missing an arm, rocketed in Roger's direction, its three remaining hooks spiralling viciously to tear him apart.

Max stabbed with the hyperblade right into the centre of the robot's metal housing. The tentacles juddered and drooped as its circuits overloaded. Max tried to free the blade again, but it was lodged fast. There was no time to waste. He let it go and swam on towards the pod.

"A fine strike, nephew," said the Professor. "Your mother would be so proud. She never knew when to give up either."

His words struck Max harder than any physical blow could. "What have you done to her?" he yelled.

The Professor only smiled. *He's just trying to make me angry*, thought Max. *I need to get inside that pod.*

Max noticed a circular hatch in the top of the pod and kicked towards it. As soon as his fingers touched the 'open' button, a shock flared across his skin and threw him backwards.

"You don't think I'm that stupid, surely?" said his uncle.

The crystal column loomed larger by the second. It must have been a thousand times wider than the biggest tree Max had ever seen, and taller even than the highest skyscraper in Aquora. Its surface glittered with a million points of diamond light.

"Max!" screamed Lia. She'd wrapped her legs around an Attack Bot, and was battering it with one of its own hooks. "Use the shell!"

The conch shell...

Max had forgotten all about it. But Lia was right. It was all they had left. As he took it out again, he saw a flicker of doubt cross the Professor's face.

"Where did you get that?" his uncle asked.

"My mother gave it to me," Max lied.

The Professor smirked. "Well, go ahead and blow it," he said. "It'll probably fry your brains, knowing your mother's foolish experiments."

There was something – some edge of worry – in his uncle's voice. *He's scared.*

"I'll take my chances," said Max, lifting the shell to his lips.

There was a sudden whirring sound. One of the panels on the pod slid back and a blaster cannon emerged. Its barrel adjusted, aiming itself at Max's head.

Zap!

Max ducked as the blaster beam fizzled a

finger's breadth past his nose. Another blaster
emerged from the other side of the pod, and
the Professor was frantically levering on two
control sticks, trying to get the perfect shot.

Zap! Zap! Zap!

Max jerked in the water as the blaster

beams scorched past him. One caught his tunic and singed the sleeve. He snatched his arm away, letting go of the conch.

He's trying to stop me blowing it!

The shell was floating away. He'd never reach it without getting several holes burned through his flesh.

"Enough!" said the Professor. "You won't ruin my..."

A seaquake shook them all, and the pod juddered up and down. Dorminus lurched towards the crystal column until it completely filled the water on one side, a wall of sheer grey. Max took his chance and darted for the conch.

"Leave it!" said the Professor.

"Never!" said Max.

He grabbed hold of the conch, but as he did so, something gripped both his arms from behind. Max tried to turn, but couldn't.

An Attack Bot held him fast. The two blasters on the pod shifted slightly, one aimed at his head and the other at his heart.

"I should've done this a long time ago," said the Professor, thumbs hovering over the triggers. "You'll never meet your mother now."

Max closed his eyes and gritted his teeth.

"Hey, Prof!" said a voice. "Not so fast!"

The Professor jumped in his chair, head swivelling as Lia emerged on one side of the pod. Roger rose on the other. The Merryn girl took hold of one blaster cannon and yanked it around, while Roger pulled the second away with his hook.

Zap! Zap! The blaster beams fired off aimlessly.

Max slammed an elbow into the Attack Bot, and wriggled one hand free. He put the conch shell to his lips and blew.

CHAPTER NINE

TRAIL OF DESTRUCTION

Max wasn't sure what he expected, but he was still taken aback by the sound that came out of the shell.

Beautiful music soared through the water – half sea-flute lullaby, half whalesong. His mother must have fitted the shell with some serious tech, because it was deafening. It seemed to fill Max's head and threaten to explode it.

The Attack Bot behind him flailed and

fizzed, then sank down through the water. Max saw Lia and Roger let go of the blasters and clamp their hands over their ears. Even the Professor looked terrified. Spike shook his nose sword from side to side, and Rivet's alarm signals flashed crazily and his ears retracted. Only Ko and the other Sea Ghosts seemed to be unaffected.

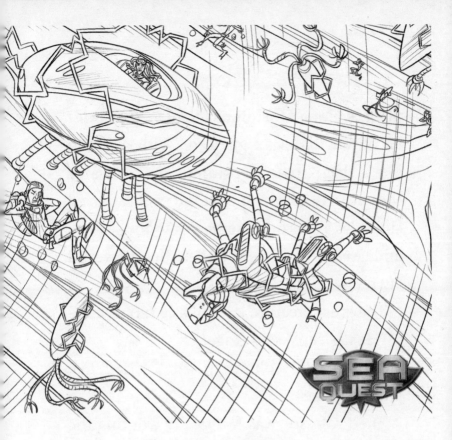

At last the sound died, leaving the water full of stirring echoes. Dull pops reached Max's ears. He turned and saw the remaining Attack Bots spouting smoke as their circuits overloaded. They sank like stones, trailing their grappling hooks. The Sea Ghosts raised their arms and cheered.

Trails of smoke rose from the electric shock

devices along Dorminus's flanks. *They must be blown too*, Max guessed. With a sound like a deep groan, Dorminus sank towards the ocean floor. Great clouds of sand sprayed sideways as his body settled onto the seabed, and weeds flattened under the powerful current.

The great creature lay still as a mountain.

"He's asleep!" said Roger.

"The crystal column is safe!" cried Lia, patting Spike.

The Professor was frantically working the controls of his pod, but it creaked and smoked just like all the other electrical equipment. One by one, the lights on his control panel died out. "What's wrong with this thing?" he hissed.

"The sound of the conch must have knocked out the power," said Max. "You're not getting away this time."

The Professor's face was white behind the viewing panel. "You'll never take me." He pulled a visor over his face, then heaved on a lever. The entrance panel exploded off the pod, then the Professor shot through, still strapped to his seat. The gills on his neck flared as he breathed water, then boosters on the underside of the chair sent him hurtling

through the water like a comet. A few seconds later, he was lost in a distant trail of bubbles.

"We should chase him," said Lia.

Max stared after the rapidly departing Professor, but then his eyes fell on Rivet. His dogbot was floating upside down, all four legs stiff. His lights were dark, his power cut. His body butted lifelessly against Dorminus's back.

"The Professor can wait," Max said, swimming quickly to Rivet's side. He opened the panel on Riv's neck. The central power generator was black and smoking. Max switched to battery back-up, and rebooted the circuits. It would have to do until he could get some tools to repair the damage.

Test lights blinked on, and Rivet's eyes flashed red, then green.

"Abalone!" he barked in a loud voice. "Anchovy! Angler fish..."

"Oh dear," said Max. "He's going over his vocab circuits. It could take a while."

"Barracuda! Bass! Belt fish! Bream..."

"Can't you at least turn it down?" asked Lia.

Max fiddled with a dial and Rivet's voice dropped. "Carp!" he muttered, more quietly

now. "Catfish! Cod! Cuttlefish..."

Max switched off the sound completely, and Roger breathed a sigh of relief.

Thank you, said a voice. *Thank you*, repeated a hundred more.

Max saw that they were suddenly surrounded by the Sea Ghosts, whose shimmering forms lit up the ocean in a green glow. Ko and his mother floated at the centre.

"We should be thanking you," said Max. "You came to our rescue."

"You and your mother give Sea Ghosts braveness," said Ko. "Now we not afraid for future."

My mother, thought Max, clutching the conch shell tighter. She'd saved them all, though she didn't know it. It was almost as if she were here herself, watching over him. Had she known that one day Max would follow in her footsteps?

Lia must have known what Max was thinking, because she squeezed his shoulder. "Come on," she said. "We don't want to wake you-know-who again!"

The following day, Max and Lia waited at the gates of Spectron. The Sea Ghosts had gathered to see them off, and Allis floated beside them in the water. Rivet and Spike were darting in and out of portholes, chasing each other's tails.

They'd all had a good night's sleep in the luxury cabins of an abandoned cruise ship, after a splendid feast of seaweed cakes and green algae mousse. From their scavenged stores, the Sea Ghosts had even found some old tins of sausages from the world above the sea. The taste reminded Max of home.

Max scanned the city. Half of it was in

ruins, brought down when Dorminus had stirred under the foundations. "What will you do?" he asked Allis.

"We rebuild," said Ko's mother with a shrug. "In Spectron, nothing is wasted."

Rivet shot through a porthole and paddled to Max's side.

"Where's Roger?" said Lia.

Max shrugged. The pirate had drunk a lot of rum the night before, so he was probably nursing a sore head. Max turned up Riv's volume, but he still hadn't finished his vocab checks: "Salmon! Sardine! Skate! Squid! Starfish! Sturgeon..." Max turned him down again.

Farewell, Max of Aquora and Lia of Sumara, said the old Sea Ghost nearest to them. *We wish you a safe journey to the world above.*

"Thank you," said Max. Ko peeped shyly from behind the old man.

"Come here!" said Lia. As Ko emerged she threw her arms around him and planted a kiss on his cheek. His green outline darkened in what must have been a Sea Ghost blush.

"I decide," he said. "Ko come with you. Keep Max and Lia safe."

"Of course!" said Max. "If your people allow it."

"Go forth, young Ko," said the old Sea Ghost.

Ko climbed into the buggy with Max.

"Ahoy there!" said a voice. Roger stuck his head from the cabin window of an old fishing boat, then zoomed towards them. "Arrr! You weighing anchor without a goodbye to Cap'n Roger?"

Max shook his head. "You're really taking this pirate thing to heart, aren't you?"

"What d'ye mean?" said Roger. "Arrr!"

"Never mind," said Max, smiling. "Try to

stay out of trouble, Roger."

"So I will! The same to you, young Master Max. Now, I've one or two things to do and one or two people to see but perhaps we'll

meet again one day. May the seas be kind t'ye!"

Max shook hands with the pirate, waved to Allis and her people, and pressed the throttle pedal of the buggy. It shot forward, carrying them away from the Sea Ghost city.

Farewell, Spectron...

CHAPTER TEN

HOMECOMING

Max's heart filled with wonder to see Sumara again. The towering coral structures and the seaweed pennants fluttered in the gentle currents.

Ko had found a shortcut out of the Cavern of Ghosts. They'd travelled for a long time through a narrow rocky tunnel, sloping upwards. But now, at last, they were back.

As they swam towards the Merryn palace, guards armed with spears raced towards them and drifted in the water, blocking their path.

"You can't bring his sort in here!" said one, pointing his spear at Ko. Max had forgotten how much the Merryn distrusted the Sea Ghosts.

"You can't tell me what to do," said Lia, brushing the weapon aside. "I am your Princess, remember? Now take me to my father."

The guards looked at each other uncertainly. "Yes, Your Highness," the second guard grumbled.

Max and his companions were led by the guards down the main street of Sumara, under the gleaming Arch of Peace. Ko's outline was trembling a little, but Lia smiled at him and told him not to be afraid. Merryn folk moved aside to let them pass, staring and muttering.

"I thought she'd run away," Max heard, and "Is that a Sea Ghost?"

Lia left Spike outside and the guards took them into the palace. They swam up a set of stone steps and across a bridge into King Salinus's private chamber. Lia's father was studying a map of the oceans.

The King's turquoise eyes widened as he saw them approach. "Lia! Is that really you? I thought you were... We looked everywhere..." His voice was choked with emotion.

Lia swam to her father and they embraced. When King Salinus opened his eyes again, they landed on Ko and narrowed in suspicion. "What is the meaning of this?"

"Ko's our friend," said Lia. "We saved his life from the Professor, and he saved ours in return."

"But he's a...a..."

"A Sea Ghost, yes," said Max. "But we've been to Spectron and they treated us kindly. It was Ko who warned us about the Professor.

Without him, Sumara would be nothing but dust now."

King Salinus released his daughter. "What do you mean? We felt terrible earthquakes. Were they the work of the Professor?"

"It's a lot to explain," said Lia. "You'd better sit down."

It was a long time before Lia had finished her tale. Max filled in parts too, about all their adventures, and the four terrible Robobeasts that the Professor had unleashed on the Cavern of Ghosts. Rivet, his circuits now functioning again, barked the occasional word like "Jellyfish!", "Scared!" and "Big bang!"

"Roger says Dorminus will probably never wake again," said Lia.

"And you trust the word of this pirate?" said her father suspiciously.

"Well, he's not really a pirate," she said. "Not exactly."

"He certainly sounds like one. Didn't you say he had a hook for a hand, and an eye patch?"

"We've learned to trust a lot of people we were suspicious of at first," said Max, glancing at Ko.

King Salinus nodded. "Yes, I fear we have misjudged the Sea Ghost people. For too long, we've had no contact with Spectron. But that will change now. We will send ambassadors. Sea Ghosts will once again be the friends of the Merryn. But first of all, I propose a feast. To celebrate my daughter's safe return and the courage of Spectron!"

Another feast! thought Max. *I'm not sure my stomach can handle it...*

But Ko smiled and bowed. "Thank you, Your Highness."

● ● ●

Glowing fish swam among the Merryn like moving lanterns, every colour of the rainbow. Pipes, horns and chimes played as Max whirled Lia around. One of the Merryn musicians was beating a drum in quick time.

"You know," Lia said, "you're not a bad dancer, for a Breather."

Max laughed. "It's funny. Up there, I had two left feet!"

The song finished and partners drifted apart. Max and Lia swam to the edge of the banquet tables.

"It's good to be home," said Lia.

"Yes," said Max, without even thinking. "Well, what I mean is...it's good to be back here in Sumara."

He cast a glance upwards, towards the surface.

"Are you feeling homesick?" Lia asked. "Do you miss your father?"

Max thought of Aquora – the amazing boats and submersibles in its harbours, the soaring buildings, the sound of the waves hitting the city's walls and the feel of the wind in his hair. He wondered what his dad was doing at that very moment. Probably working late, making sure the city was safe. He felt a rush of pride and a pang of loneliness at the same time.

"Yes, I miss it," he said, "but my place is here now. I've had the Merryn Touch too long to go back."

"Like your uncle," Lia said grimly. "Do you think we'll ever see him again?"

Max nodded. "I don't think my uncle is the sort of man who gives up. But I'll be ready."

The music had started again – a slower tune, with just pipes.

"Can I have this dance?"

They both turned and saw Ko's semi-transparent form. He held out a hand to Lia.

"Of course," she said with a smile. "Just don't tread on my fins."

Max watched them whisk off towards the dancing area. He sat on a smooth boulder, and stared out past the coral towers of Sumara into the open sea. His hand crept inside his suit and found the conch shell. Until recently the only link he'd had with his mother had been dim memories. Now, as those memories faded further every day, he had this mysterious object. Despite all his doubts, she had made it for a good purpose. She had wanted to protect Dorminus, an innocent creature of the sea, against her brother.

Of course I can't go back home. Not while she might still be out there.

Whether she was dead or alive, he would never stop searching for her.

Don't miss Max's next Sea Quest adventure,
when he faces

TETRAX
THE SWAMP CROCODILE

SEA QUEST ®

Look out for all the books in
Sea Quest Series 3:

THE PRIDE OF BLACKHEART

TETRAX THE SWAMP CROCODILE
NEPHRO THE ICE LOBSTER
FINARIA THE SAVAGE SEA SNAKE
CHAKROL THE OCEAN HAMMER

OUT IN MARCH 2014!

Don't miss the
BRAND NEW
Special Bumper Edition:

STENGOR
THE CRAB MONSTER

978 1 40831 852 2

OUT IN NOVEMBER 2013

WIN AN EXCLUSIVE
GOODY BAG

In every Sea Quest book the Sea Quest logo is hidden in one of the pictures. Find the logos in books 5–8, make a note of which pages they appear on and go online to enter the competition at

www.seaquestbooks.co.uk

Each month we will put all of the correct entries into a draw and select one winner to receive a special Sea Quest goody bag.

You can also send your entry on a postcard to:

Sea Quest Competition, Orchard Books,
338 Euston Road, London, NW1 3BH

Don't forget to include your name and address!

GOOD LUCK

Closing Date: December 30th 2013

IF YOU LIKE SEA QUEST, YOU'LL LOVE **BEAST QUEST!**

FREE COLLECTOR CARDS INSIDE!

Series 1: COLLECT THEM ALL!

An evil wizard has enchanted the magical beasts of Avantia. Only a true hero can free the beasts and save the land. Is Tom the hero Avantia has been waiting for?

978 1 84616 483 5

978 1 84616 482 8

978 1 84616 484 2

978 1 84616 486 6

978 1 84616 485 9

978 1 84616 487 3

DON'T MISS THE
BRAND NEW SERIES OF:

Series 14: THE CURSED DRAGON

978 1 40832 920 7

978 1 40832 921 4

978 1 40832 922 1

978 1 40832 923 8

OUT IN JANUARY 2014!